FACING LIFE'S CHALLENGES
IN TIMES OF
STRUGGLE

*A Reimaging of the Jacob-Joseph
Saga in Genesis 27-46*

The Rev. Debra Moody Bass, Ph.D

WESTBOW
PRESS®
A DIVISION OF THOMAS NELSON
& ZONDERVAN

WestBow Press books may be ordered through booksellers or by contacting:

WestBow Press
A Division of Thomas Nelson & Zondervan
1663 Liberty Drive
Bloomington, IN 47403
www.westbowpress.com
844-714-3454

Scripture taken from the King James Version of the Bible.

ISBN: 978-1-6642-4405-4 (sc)
ISBN: 978-1-6642-4404-7 (e)

Print information available on the last page.

WestBow Press rev. date: 09/01/2021

CONTENTS

INTRODUCTION

In Genesis 27-50 we find the Jacob-Joseph story. It is one of the more familiar stories in the Old Testament. The family dynamics and drama are classic and timeless for every new generation.

Throughout these chapters we encounter sibling rivalry, in-law deception, jealousy, revenge, fertility issues, forgiveness, cultural disputes, reconciliation and finally family reunion. Many of life's challenges are included in these chapters and somewhat addressed through theological interpretation, which gives everything meaning.

The moral of the story is that life is full of challenges, but with God on our side we can be victorious. The end usually justifies the means in Genesis. For even when life comes at us with ill intent, God can use it for our good. We only need to focus on our spiritual gifts to empower us and give us the victory over the things that will try to defeat us.

This book takes the Jacob-Joseph saga into the 21st century. The narrative is similar but the content has taken on a more modern and relevant flavor. Jacob leaves home and drives to his Uncle Laban's home. Jacob meets Rachel at a convenience store, instead of a well to water sheep. Jacob is adopted not Laban's biological child. A Pharaoh replaces a governor. Joseph is falsely arrested instead of sold into slavery by his brothers to a Midian caravan. The "dream" component of the Jacob-Joseph saga continues to serve as the central motif and the gift that eventually saved Joseph's life and reunited the family.

So there are twists and turns and substitutes throughout the saga but biblical readers will recognize the classical thread that runs through both stories. Enjoy the ride and be blessed!

CHAPTER 1

Jacob Faces The Challenge Of Leaving Home (Genesis 27-37)

JACOB LEAVES HOME: (GENESIS 27)

J acob was on his way to visit his Uncle Laban because he was having problems at home with his big brother. *(Gen 27:41)* They had a falling out over their father's inheritance. Rebekah, Jacob's mother and Isaac's wife, suggested Jacob leave town under the guise that she did not want him to marry one of the daughters of Canaan, to find a wife from her family lineage until his brother cooled off (she felt the need to protect Jacob from the wrath of his twin brother Esau). So Jacob packed up his car and left his childhood home in Canaan and traveled to Haran. Jacob expected his journey to be long, hot, and uneventful. Boy was he in for a surprise! The drive was about 7 hours long, so about half way, he stopped at a hotel to rest. He had never traveled that far away from home before.

As Jacob slept through the night, he began to dream about people climbing up and down ladders. *(Gen 28:10-12)* When he finally awakened, he was perplexed about what the dream could mean. Realizing he still had a ways to go to get to his uncle's house, Jacob gathered his stuff and got in his car to finish the trip. Haran was his mother's ancestral home. This intrigued him.

As Jacob was driving, the voice of God spoke to him. Jacob had never heard God's voice before so he thought it was some static in the car radio. God called out Jacob's name a second time and told Jacob to worship him. Jacob thought he was losing his mind or having a heat stroke so he pulled over to the side of the road.

Jacob's mom, Rebekah, was a very religious woman so Jacob was raised in the church. Once he pulled over in a McDonald's parking lot, God called his name again and told Jacob he was chosen to be the leader of his family and to carry on the blessings promised to his grandfather, Abraham. God promised to be with Jacob and protect him but he had to swear allegiance to the God of his ancestors. *(Gen 28:13-15)*

Jacob was hesitant but could not resist the offer God was making to him in lieu of his family issues. Jacob agreed to be in partnership with the God of his ancestors. The conversation ended and Jacob was back on the road again heading towards Haran. *(Gen 28:20-22)*

Jacob had never been to Haran before and his car did not have a GPS so as he got closer to the exit for Haran, he stopped to get gas, stretch his legs, maybe get something cool to drink, and ask for directions to his uncle's house. It was at this gas station that his life was about to change forever.

JACOB MEETS HIS FUTURE BRIDE (GENESIS 29:9-12)

As Jacob entered the service station convenience store, a beautiful tall dark hair, slim, young woman was exiting the store with a cup of coffee in her hand. Jacob fell in love at first sight! He approached the young woman and introduced himself. She smiled and said her name was Rachael. After sharing some small talk, Jacob finally got up enough nerve to ask Rachel for her phone number. She said no, that her father would not approve of her giving her phone number to a stranger.

So they said their goodbyes and went their separate ways, or so they thought. After getting directions from the cashier (why didn't he ask Rachael?) he went on his merry way, heading straight to his Uncle Laban's house. He was getting hungry so he hoped he would arrive by dinnertime. About 30 minutes later in a rural area, Jacob drove up to a dirt road and to the front of the house. According to the directions he received at the convenience store, this should be his e's residence.

Jacob got out of the car, stretched a little bit, checked out his appearance in the rear view mirror, smoothed out his clothes, and walked up to the front door of the farmhouse. He wanted to make a good first impression. Jacob knocked on the red farmhouse door. At first there was no answer. He knocked again, harder this time. There was no doorbell in sight. Finally the door began to slowly open and to his surprise, Rachael, the young woman he met at the gas station, was standing right in the path of the doorway.

Jacob spoke first. "Hi. I know this seems awkward since we just met 30 minutes ago at the gas station, but I am looking for my uncle. His name is Laban and I was told he lives here." Rachel smiled and told Joseph that Laban was her father and was out in the field tending to the livestock.

Jacob invited him in and offered him something to drink while they wait for her father to return. Jacob accepted the hospitality and she served him a cold tall glass of sweet tea. Jacob was very thirsty from the long ride and forgot to buy something to drink at the gas station. He was so taken aback by Rachel's beauty that he forgot all about his thirst.

Jacob and Rachel tried to engage in some small talk. Rachel was very shy and was not use to entertaining men in her father's house. She was hoping he father would return from the field sooner than later. Yet the chemistry between them could not be denied.

JACOB MEET HIS UNCLE LABAN (GENESIS 29:13-14)

About an hour passed and finally Laban returned from the fields, smelling of animal hide, and covered in dust and dirt. At first he was shocked to see Rachael entertaining a strange man in his house. She knew the rules. Whoever this man was he better have a good explanation for why he was able to convince Rachel to let him in his home. But before Laban could speak, Jacob approached him with his hand extended to introduce himself. "Hi uncle Laban. I am your sister Rebekah's baby boy. We have never met, but my mom sent me to visit with you because of some trouble back home. She thought it would be best if I left town for awhile until things settled down and tempers cooled."

Laban took a long hard look at Jacob. He had never seen Jacob in person, but did know his sister had a set of twins about 25 years ago. Laban and Rebekah were not close because he did not want her to marry Isaac and leave the family home. They had not spoken to each other in 30 years! Now here was her grown son standing in his living room, asking to stay awhile.

The scowl on Laban's face slowly turned to a smile as he approached Jacob to embrace him and welcome him to the family. If he needed a place to stay he was welcome. That's what family is for! So Laban and Jacob sat down and talked about the living arrangements. Laban had a large farm with sheep and goats. He would hire his nephew to work for him and earn his room and board. Jacob was more than happy to accept this arrangement since he left home with only what he could put in his car. Rebekah gave him some money she had saved from groceries, but that only covered his gas to get to Haran. Now he was flat broke. He did not know what he would have done if his uncle had rejected him and sent him on his way. Then Jacob realized that God was keeping his promise to protect him.

Laban had a guesthouse behind the main house and told Jacob that would be his new home while he was in town. Laban gave Jacob the keys and Jacob walked out the front door of the house and walked toward his new home. As he walked out to the porch, he turned around and said to his uncle, "Thanks, I won't let you down." But Rachel had a devilish grin on her face as she watched Jacob walk away. You could see on her face what she was thinking. "Cousin or not, this man is a good catch!" After all, Rachael was adopted so they were not blood relatives.

ONE YEAR LATER, A BRIDE PRICE IS SET (GENESIS 29:18-20)

Jacob and Rachel began dating a few months after he arrived in Haran. They had her father's blessing. When Jacob was ready to ask for Rachael's hand in marriage, they approached Laban with a plan on how he would work for a set number of years to pay the dowry price for Rachael to her father. Jacob did not have a lot of money, just the little he was able to save after he paid Laban room and board. He was allowed to eat at the family table so he did not have to buy groceries. He was thankful for that at least.

Jacob and Laban began to negotiate the bride price for his beloved Rachael. Laban could see how much in love they were and took advantage of the situation. He wanted to get as much free labor out of Jacob as he possibly could. His first offer was for Jacob to work 10 years. Jacob countered with 5 years. After much back and forth, they finally agreed on 7 years. In Jacob's mind, whatever it takes to be Rachael's husband was fine with him. They would continue to date and the 7 years will pass by quickly.

Finally the wedding day arrived! Rachael was going to be his bride! All was right with the world! The wedding celebration was massive and went on for 10 days. Jacob partied a little too much and was not in the best condition to greet his bride on their wedding night. As was custom, Rachael celebrated separately with her two bride's maids – her older sister Leah and her best friend Sara. She would be reunited with her groom after the ceremony, in the wedding chamber.

Jacob entered the wedding chamber first. Rachel later entered the wedding chamber escorted by her father. She was still wearing her veil and the room was very dark. The only light was the window in the door. Jacob embraced his new bride and finally was able to become one with his beloved Rachael.

THE MORNING SURPRISE (GENESIS 29:25-27)

After so much partying, the newly wedded couple decided to "sleep in". Finally, around noon and the sun outside brought some light into the room, Jacob turned to his new wife to say good morning. But to his surprise, it was not Rachael! Someone had played a bad cultural trick on him. Jacob was getting a taste of his own medicine, for the reason he had to leave home was because he tricked his brother out of his birthright and blessing as the eldest son. As a matter of fact, his name means "trickster, or deceiver." *(Gen 25-35)*

Jacob hurriedly got dressed and drove straight to his father-in-law's house to find out what happened. Laban heard Jacob coming and was ready to take on his rage and disappointment. Jacob reminded Laban that he had kept his side of the bargain. He worked 7 years for his beloved Rachael to become his wife. The woman lying next to him this morning was not Rachael, but here older sister Leah! What a dirty trick to play on your nephew, now son-in-law.

Laban was not moved by Jacob's outrage. Yes, he failed to inform Jacob of their tribal custom, which stated that the eldest daughter must marry first. Although Rachael is adopted, by law she could not marry before Leah, Laban's firstborn. Of course Laban knew he had tricked Jacob, but he had hoped that within the 7 years of courtship, some young suitor would come calling on Leah and she would marry before Rachael. However, it did not happen so Laban had to take matters into his own hands.

Rachael was very attractive, but Leah was a "plain Jane" and did not care much about frilly girly stuff. *(Gen 29:17)* Since her father had no sons, Leah took the role on and dressed in a manly way to do the work on the farm that a son would do. To most of the men in town Leah was "one of the boys." They did not see her in a romantic way.

Well Jacob thought this had nothing to do with him and his agreement to marry Rachael after 7 years of working for his uncle. He left Laban's house in a fury and packed up his stuff to depart from Haran, leaving his new bride in her father's care. When Laban heard Jacob was leaving his employ, he hurried to Jacob's house to plead with him to stay.

Jacob would not here any of it! He had made up his mind and was going to head to the nearest town away from Laban and his trickery. However, Laban was aware that Jacob was anointed by God and that his prosperity over the past 7 years had everything to do with Jacob's anointing and not his own business sense. He had to do something to get Jacob to stay. Knowing how much Jacob still loved Rachael he quickly came up with a new agreement. He offered Jacob Rachael's hand in marriage since their community practiced polygamy. The wedding would take place in two weeks (out of respect for Leah's feelings and the end of the honeymoon period). Yet, the bride price would be the same – 7 years of work. *(Gen 29:27)*

Jacob pondered the thought of never seeing Rachael again and it broke his heart. So again he trusted Laban and this time he had Rachael's name written on the promissory note. The first time it only said "a daughter of Laban." He was not going to be tricked again. Who knows, Laban may have some other daughters he wants to marry off. Jacob also requested the document be signed by the Elders of the community to serve as witnesses to insure there would be no trickery this time.

_____

JACOB AND RACHAEL BECOME ONE (GENESIS 29:28)

A Month later Rachael and Jacob married in a small ceremony in the village. This was so Leah, his first wife, would not have her nose rubbed in Jacob's rejection of her. In this way she could preserve her dignity.

_____

LEAH GIVES JACOB MANY SONS (GENESIS 29:31-35)

Procreation was the primary function of women in the village of Haran. By law even though Jacob did not love Leah, as his first wife, he still had to perform his conjugal duty every 30 days. So God blessed

Leah and she was very fertile. She was able to bear many children for Jacob, in hope that this would cause Jacob to love her. She gave birth to 5 sons. Sons were considered a blessing in their village. But because Jacob did not love Leah, he did not show affection towards her children. Leah named her sons according to her depression and sadness in a loveless marriage. Jacob was not trying to be hurtful he just did not love Leah nor asked her to be his wife. It was an arranged marriage that he wanted no part of. His heart only belonged to Rachael.

After a few years, Rachael still had not produced any children for Jacob. This caused Rachael great frustration and despair as she watched her sister Leah bear sons for Jacob. In her village, a woman's worth was mostly connected to the male children she birthed. This insured her husband's legacy.

Rachael eventually went to the doctor for tests but he diagnosed her as barren, infertile. Rachael then decided to take matters in her own hands and asked her maid to be a surrogate for her so she could give Jacob a child. Rachael also felt in competition with Jacob's first wife – Leah. Although his marital contract with Leah obligated one night a month to give Leah her conjugal rights, it was enough for Leah to continually get pregnant and birth sons for her husband. It was a role she could not yet play in her relationship. She thought the town gossip among the women was about her.

RACHAEL GIVES BIRTH (GENESIS 30:22-24)

Rachael prayed to God to open her womb. After a few years, Rachael finally was able to conceive and give Jacob a son, and they named him Joseph. Just as the birth of Joseph was a miracle, so too would Joseph's life be to those around him. This miracle baby was Rachael's dream come true. Did I say, "dream?" That word would become the center of Joseph's destiny.

Because Jacob loved Rachael so deeply, he cherished Joseph more than hi other children. Playing favorites in a large family situation never ends well. To make matters worse, Rachael gave birth to a second son, Benjamin, but died later after complications in delivery. This was a devastating blow to Jacob who loved Rachael more than his own life. *(Gen 35:16-29)*

Now all Jacob had left of his beloved Rachael were their two sons together – Joseph and Benjamin. He kept them close to him and showed favoritism toward them over the other children. As the children – 12 in all – grew older, so did their resentment towards Rachael's two children. However, because of Joseph's special gift he felt the brunt of their jealousy. *(Gen 37:3-4)*

CHAPTER 2

Joseph Faces The Challenge Of Sibling Rivalry Gone Wrong (Genesis 37-39)

JOSEPH'S DREAMS BEGIN (GENESIS 37:5-11)

Joseph was a light sleeper because he was a dreamer. Dreams about his family and his life in general consumed his sub-conscience as he tried to sleep through the night. Joseph usually kept his dreams to himself, but on one occasion he decided to share one of his dreams with his brothers. That did not go well. *(Gen 37:8-11)*

In the dream, Joseph was appointed CEO of his fathers' farming business. Jacob had over 200 acres of farmland that included a 1000 head of cattle, 100 sheep, and 100 goats. Joseph's older brothers worked the farm on a daily basis. His brothers knew the business better than Joseph and was angry when they found out Joseph would be their boss. At one of the meetings all the workers were told to recognize Joseph as their boss and give him a standing ovation.

At this point in the dream, Joseph woke up. The next day his father's asked him to visit his brothers to check up on their productivity. His siblings saw him as a spy for their father and resented his visits. Their reaction to his visits grew more and more hostile and eventually they could no longer hide their anger.

As most of us who come from a large family can attest to, our parents were not always successful at hiding who was their favorite child. Sometimes it was unintentional. There was just a personality similarity or a skill and hobby shared between parent and child. Often the eldest child was given the responsibility of caring for the younger siblings, especially if both parents worked. In this situation, parents relied heavily on the eldest child to discipline, cook, help with homework, assign chores, even counsel and give love advice to their younger siblings.

This role can easily be mistaken as a "favorite child" label, when in reality it was just a practical and physical decision. It allowed the family to function more smoothly while the parents worked to support the family. However, this also caused the parents to relate more so with the firstborn, and seemingly ignore the younger children. This was not the case with Jacob and Joseph's relationship. Although he was the firstborn of Rachael, he was number 11 in Jacob's children line-up. Joseph was his favorite and everybody knew it.

_____

JOSEPH IS CHALLENGED (GENESIS 37:12-36)

On one sunny day in May, Jacob asked Joseph to go and check on his brothers. Joseph enjoyed interacting with his brothers and loved them very much. He was not aware of the depth of his siblings hate for him. They saw Joseph as a tatter-tale and wanted no part of his visits on their Father's behalf. *(Gen 37:12-14)*

The night before this visit, Joseph had another dream about his family. Again Joseph was the CEO of the farming business his father started after Jacob cut ties with his father-in-law Laban. In the dream his family were bowing down to him in total submission to his power and authority over them. *(Gen 37:7)* Since he was on his way to visit his brothers, in his naivete` he decided to share his dream with his brothers.

Yet, not all Joseph's brothers hated him. Some were just annoyed about his perceived favoritism and others thought he was an arrogant know it all. But the two that despised him were able to convince the others to teach Joseph a lesson the next time he came to visit them in the fields. On this day they would get that opportunity to teach Joseph a lesson he would never forget, and break their father's heart in the process.

Joseph was in a happy place on this day. Earlier in the day, his father presented him with a beautiful pair of new cowboy boots and a new cowboy hat. He decided to wear them when he went to visit his brothers in the field. This was not a good idea. Joseph had no clue about how his brothers really felt about him, nor that they were plotting his demise. *(Gen 37:3)*

The brothers saw Joseph coming towards them on his horse. As Joseph got closer, they noticed his new cowboy hat. Then when he got off the horse, they noticed his new cowboy boots. They chose not to give Joseph the satisfaction of noticing his hat and boots. But Joseph was determined to show off his new hat and cowboy boots. This made two of his brothers so angry that their first thought was how to get rid of Joseph. But Reuben, the oldest, calmed them down and instead suggested they put Joseph in the bottom of the well to teach him a lesson. *(Gen 37:21-24)*

The brothers agreed. However, the narrative changes when Joseph's only ally, Reuben, left the camp in order to check on some supplies that were scheduled for delivery. This gave some of the brothers the opportunity to inflict a harsher punishment on Joseph. *(Gen 38:29)*

JOSEPH GOES TO JAIL (GENESIS 38:27-28)

As they were trying to figure out what to do about Joseph, a police car drove up to their camp. One officer got out of the car and approached two of the brothers standing in front of the barn. The officer greeted them and said he was looking for a young man who was wanted for sexual assault against a female neighbor. They had him in the squad car but somehow he was able to get loose and when they stopped at a red light, he opened the door and ran off.

This gave one of the brothers an idea to fix Joseph for good. So he told the officer that they saw a suspicious looking young man on their property earlier and they chased him. In the chase the young man fell in their well so they left him there. They were just about to call the police when the officer drove up.

The officer asked the brothers to show him the well location. When they arrived at the well the officer let down a rope to help Joseph get out. The well was deep, dark and damp so Joseph could not see the officer. He thought it was one of his brothers. In addition he was suffering from hyperthermia because the well water was freezing and he had been in the well now for several hours.

The officer arrested Joseph on the spot. Joseph was confused and did not know what was going on. His brothers pretended they did not know who Joseph was and allowed the officer to put Joseph in the back seat of the police. The officer drove straight to the police station. He was not about to lose another suspect. As the officer drove away, one of the brothers laughed and said, "Let him dream himself out of that situation."

When they arrived at the police station, Joseph was not concerned. He knew this was a joke his brothers were playing on him and soon they would come down to the station and straighten everything out. This was all a case of mistaken identity. People knew Joseph in the farm community, but not so much in the city. Joseph was a homebody at his father's urging, so he did not wander away too far from his father's house.

Joseph tried to explain what was going on, but after the officer was embarrassed about the real inmate escaping from the back of his squad car he was substituting one guilty inmate for an innocent bystander. But Joseph still was not worried. He knew God was on his side and believed that his brothers would come to their senses and vouch for his innocence. Yet, hours later, the brothers still had not come. So Joseph was booked as a suspect and locked up in the city jail until he could be cleared and his true identity established. *(Gen 39:1-3)*

CHAPTER 3

Joseph's Challenge Takes A Turn For The Worse (Genesis 37, 39)

JACOB SUFFERS ANOTHER LOSS (GENESIS 37:23)

It was getting late in the evening and Jacob was starting to worry about why Joseph had not returned home from visiting his brothers in the field. He called in his other sons and they claimed Joseph never showed up and they had not seen him all day. They had no idea where Joseph could be. Reuben decided to keep quiet until he could figure out what his brothers did to Joseph.

This of course, was Jacob's worse nightmare coming true – losing Joseph, his firstborn son with his now deceased Rachael. It was not like Joseph to stay away so long without contacting him. What could have possibly happened to his beloved favorite child? Would he ever see his precious Joseph again? Jacob falls into a deep depression. For months Jacob was inconsolable. Yet, secretly in his heart, he always held on to the hope that he would see Joseph again. Twenty-years later that hope will become a reality.

When the sun had set and the full moon was high in the sky, Joseph realized that this act on his brother's part was more serious than he thought. Surely by morning he would be back in his father's house, with his baby brother Benjamin, and in his warm bed. Joseph settled down for the night on the hard cot in his jail cell. Soon he drifted off to sleep and the dreams started to reveal his future.

Joseph has the same dream again about holding the CEO position at a large mega-farm organization. But this time it was not his father's company by his father's competition! In the dream, Joseph hired his brothers to work for him and moved them to the city of Bethel. In Bethel, there was a large manufacturing factory. There were over 500 workers employed to work the farm and take care of the herds.

As Joseph was about to address the board members at their annual meeting, he was awakened by the sound of a tin cup hitting the metal bars of his jail cell. Startled he jumped up and realized he was still in jail! This was not a dream but his new reality. The officer told Joseph to get up and come with him. Joseph thought that finally someone was coming to bail him out. Maybe it was his father. However, to his surprise and disappointment, the officer escorted him on to a bus along with other inmates. What was happening? This joke had gone too far! He tried to communicate his circumstances to the officers but they would hear none of it. They had heard every innocent excuse in the book.

What was Joseph to do? What recourse did he have? It was obvious at this point that he was being falsely accused of a crime he did not commit. What was the charge? Why did he not have an attorney or even a phone call? He could have contacted his father and all this would have been over with. Joseph knew this was a bad situation about to get worse.

GOD ASSURES JOSEPH OF HIS PRESENCE AND PROTECTION (GENESIS 39)

While riding on the bus in hand cuffs, heading to God knows where, Joseph begins to pray to God for clarity and understanding. What was happening and why was God allowing this to happen? God promised to protect him. He thought about how worried his father must be not hearing from him for 24 hours. Truly this must be a bad dream and he was going to wake up any minute.

As the bus pulled into the gates of the state penitentiary God spoke to Joseph. God reassured Joseph that he was with him and was in control of the situation. Joseph needed only to trust that God had a purpose for Joseph's plight. God would be Joseph's protector at every turn while he was in prison. Joseph need not worry about his wellbeing.

After a week in the state penitentiary, Jacob knew his brothers were never going to show up. This was now his place to do ministry. God was using him to teach others about his existence. Eventually, Joseph was assigned a lawyer, but his case was a cover-up and he went to trial on the false testimony of a woman who accused Joseph of sexual assault. The judge believed the woman because she was the wife of a prominent politician. *Gen 39:7-19)*

Yet, because Joseph was an immigrant from the country of Canaan, he was convicted by public opinion. Joseph remembered God's words to him and did not appeal the verdict. All of this was a part of God's plan. He did not understand it, but he trusted God unconditionally.

Joseph had the favor of God over his life so he was well liked by the prison administration. *(Gen 39:21-23)* He was put in positions of leadership over other inmates because of his gentle and comforting tone with the other inmates. Joseph always listened when they came to him with their problems and complaints. With his gift of interpretation of dreams, he often settled disputes between the inmates and the officers as well. Joseph was the warden's favorite and was often used by the warden to keep the jail peaceful.

CHAPTER 4

Joseph's Challenge Is Met By His Gift Of Interpretation (Genesis 40)

NEW INMATES ARRIVE (GENESIS 40:1-4)

Soon after Joseph arrived at the jail in Jerusalem, two high profile persons were brought to the prison. They were the governor's lawyer and his chief of staff. They both were accused of participating in a plot to overthrow the state government. They did not agree with the governor's new tax plan, which would have placed higher taxes on the wealthy.

Joseph sought them out once they were fingerprinted, had their mug shots taken, and provided orange prison jumpsuits. Joseph sensed their fear and trepidation about their new living quarters. He wanted to ease their discomfort by sharing with them his experience at the jail. He assured these two men that if they followed the rules and stayed out of trouble, their time served will go by quickly.

Each prisoner is assigned a job to do. This helped the time pass each day and kept the prison running smoothly. Jobs ranged from clerical to janitorial, to laundry duty and kitchen service. Joseph was appointed over the inmates to make sure they completed their jobs on time.

JOSEPH INTERPRETS THE INMATES' DREAMS (GENESIS 40:5-19)

Joseph treated each inmate with respect and was well liked. On one occasion as some of the inmates were gathered for the dinner meal, the governor's lawyer began to share his experience the night before while sleeping. The lawyer had a dream that caused him great concern because he did not know what it meant. Joseph listened attentively to the details of the dream as the lawyer spoke. In the lawyer's dream he was in the courthouse standing before a judge defending the governor against a bribery charge. Then the judge stood up and walked out of the courtroom. At this point the lawyer said he woke up.

Joseph was praying the whole time the lawyer was talking, asking God to reveal the interpretation to him. He told the lawyer that God had spoken to him and that the dream meant he would be released from prison and found not guilty. The lawyer was ecstatic over Joseph's interpretation and contacted his family immediately to encourage them.

In return for his interpretation, Joseph asked the lawyer for one favor. When he was released to please put a good word in for him to the governor. He shared with the lawyer his own story about how he was arrested under false pretenses and set up by his brothers. He never received a fair trial because the witness lied on the witness stand. She was the wife of a high profiled politician so everybody believed her testimony. The lawyer agreed that after his release he would look into Joseph's case. *(Gen 40:20-23)*

Now after the governor's lawyer received a positive interpretation of his dream from Joseph, the governor's chief of staff decided to tell his dream to Joseph. The chief of staff said that in his dream he had called a staff meeting. The meeting was scheduled to start at 9 a.m. sharp! After about 10 minutes, the chief of staff noticed nobody showed up. He gave it another 10 minutes, but still none of the governor's staff arrived.

He then decided to get up from his chair at the head of the conference table and see what was going on. Did he have the date wrong? Had the governor cancelled the meeting? Then the chief of staff decided to exit the Board Room and see for himself what the problem was. As he tried to open the conference room doom, which had been closed up to this point, it would not open. He tried several times to open the door, but to no avail. So he stared banging on the door, hoping people on the other side would come to his rescue. He knocked and yelled for over 30 minutes and still no one responded. The yelling caused him to wake up from the dream.

Just as with the lawyer's dream, Joseph prayed and listened as the chief of staff told his dream. Joseph's face was saddened when he heard the dream of the chief of staff. He knew he would not like the interpretation because it was not in his favor. He told the inmate that the door was locked and he was unable to open it because he was going to be found guilty and spend the next 20 years in jail.

This interpretation was unacceptable to the chief of staff as he insisted on his innocence. He decided not to believe Joseph. Three days later on the governor's birthday, the governor decided to grant a pardon for his lawyer (as Joseph interpreted), but said nothing about his chief of staff so he remained in prison for attempting to overthrow the state government and was eventually sentenced to 20 years.

Joseph felt hopeful that the lawyer would keep his word and help him get released from prison. Joseph felt his time behind bars had run its course and he needed to move forward in his life and be reconnected to his family. He needed to be vindicated for this trumped up charge against him. He felt in his heart that God was about to do a new thing in his life. He had not seen or heard from his family for almost 10 years! Was his father and baby brother still alive? What did they know about his disappearance? What story did his half-brothers tell their father? Joseph wondered. Joseph prayed. Joseph waited on God's next move.

CHAPTER 5

Joseph's Challenge Becomes His Blessing (Genesis 41)

THE LAWYER REMEMBERS JOSEPH'S GIFT OF INTERPRETATION (GENESIS 41:1-13)

About two years went by before any movement occurred in Joseph's situation. *(Gen 41:1)* The lawyer's promise to talk to the governor on his behalf obviously was taking longer than Joseph had hoped. Then one day out of the blue, the governor's lawyer came to the prison to visit Joseph. Joseph was very happy to see the lawyer, but what did this mean for his freedom? The lawyer told Joseph that his boss, the governor, was having problems sleeping. The governor kept having the same dream over and over again. He called in the state psychologist, hypnotists, and spiritual mediums that had in the past helped the police solve crime cases. He called some religious leaders of all faiths, but none of them could help the governor get to the meaning of this dream so he could get help and solve his insomnia. *(Gen 41:8)*

The lawyer's memory about Joseph's gift of interpretation of dreams surfaced from his subconscious. He told the governor about Joseph and the governor instructed the lawyer to bring Joseph to him ASAP! So that is why the lawyer was here. If Joseph could not help the governor with his insomnia, his job was on the line for recommending him. Joseph's gift of interpreting dreams was the governor's last resort. *(Gen 41:9-13)*

Joseph prayed and listened attentively to the lawyer's words. He agreed to go sit with the governor and help him resolve whatever inner conflicts were battling for his soul and mental state. In order to get Joseph a temporary release pass for a trip to the governor's mansion, a special release form granting permission needed to be signed by the warden.

The warden was hesitant about agreeing to this temporary release. Joseph was important to the smooth running of the prison. He was not too happy about the possibility that he would lose Joseph. The warden knew in his heart that Joseph was special and had God's favor over his life. Therefore, he finally agreed to permit this temporary release for Joseph to meet with the governor.

_____

JOSEPH'S INTERPRETATION CHANGES HIS LIFE (GENESIS 41:14-41)

A special car was sent to pick up Joseph from the prison. It had dark tinted windows and was bullet proof. Two armed guards were sent to oversee the transfer. Joseph was cleaned up with a shower and a shave so he would look presentable before the governor. Any stench of prison life was washed away as dirt on a car going through a car wash. Joseph was even given cologne to contribute to his total makeover.

The ride from the prison to the governor's mansion was an hour and a half long. Joseph was in handcuffs, but was enjoying the ride through nature. It had been a long time since Joseph was in a car. Just seeing the landscape, nature, birds, passing cars, made his heart fill with joy. Joseph was not sure what was about to happen between him and the governor, but he began to pray to God for revelation and interpretation.

In Joseph's mind he was fearful of the consequences if he was unable to accurately interpret the governor's dream. As he continued to pray while sitting handcuffed in the back seat of this black town car, Joseph allowed his mind to focus on the ride. He remembered that God told him not to be afraid of anything. Joseph knew then that his time of deliverance was about to become a reality. It was about 2 p.m. when they arrived at the mansion. Joseph was amazed at the grandeur and intricate architecture of the building. The building itself was about 150 years old, designed with European gothic architecture in mind. There were large gargoyles at the top of the four corners of the building. Joseph was very impressed. He was just a farm boy who stayed close to home most of his life. His incarceration was the longest he had ever been away from home and is father.

The two guards drove up to the front of the mansion. They got out and went to open the back door of the town car. Joseph was still handcuffed. Helping Joseph out of the car, they removed his handcuffs and gave him strict orders not to try any "funny stuff" or he would regret it. They were fully armed. Joseph got the message loud and clear, not that he would have tried to escape. He was just happy to be out in the fresh air and in new surroundings.

JOSEPH MEETS THE GOVERNOR (GENESIS 41:14)

Joseph was taken to a secret room in the basement of the mansion. It was dark and gloomy. There were no windows and the walls were painted a dark hunter green. There was a light hanging from the ceiling, a 12-foot rectangular table and three gray metal chairs arranged around the table. The room was set up as an interrogation room for sure. It looked similar to one found in a police station.

Joseph was seated at one end of the table. About 15 minutes later an older man with salt and pepper hair, a wrinkled forehead, wearing a dark blue suit, entered the room. Joseph knew it was the governor because he had seen pictures of him on the prison T.V. The governor was a little stocky, but not overweight. He wore a buttoned down white shirt with a blue and white striped tie. Joseph tried to smile but his fear was controlling his every move and emotion.

One of the secret service men who escorted the governor into the room introduced the governor to Joseph. Joseph, being a humble man and shy, just nodded in acceptance of the introduction. The governor sat down at one end of the table, opposite Joseph. He asked Joseph if he knew why he was here. Joseph nodded in affirmation. The governor then began to tell his dream to Joseph.

In the dream the governor is at a political rally giving a speech to his supporters. About half way through the speech, people begin to disappear. The governor continued talking and the more he talked the more people disappeared. At the end of his speech only he and his staff on stage remained in the room.

The governor was afraid to go to rallies after having this dream. He could not understand what this dream meant for his political future and for the safety of his supporters. Would his presence cause people to die? Was this a sign that he would not be reelected to office? Was it a symbol that his supporters no longer wanted him as their governor? He needed clarity. He needed the interpretation of this dream so he would not put those surrounded him, as well as his political base, in danger.

Joseph prayed and listened attentively to the governor's words. *(Gen 41:8)* He could see how agitated the governor became while retelling this dream. His face became pale and there were beads of sweat on his brow. There was a shaking in his voice and fear in his eyes. Joseph knew that this dream, or nightmare, was holding the governor physically and emotionally hostage. It was as if he was in prison too.

Joseph closed his eyes and began to silently pray for God's intervention and interpretation of this dream. He prayed that God would bring comfort to the governor's mind. He prayed for about 10 minutes awaiting God's response. After God revealed the meaning of this dream, Joseph spoke. This is the interpretation of the governor's dream:

The disappearing people represented those persons who would become victim of a mysterious disease. The governor was told about this disease infecting farm animals across the state. The governor too no action to protect his state from ingesting these infected animals. As more and more people fell victim and succumbed to this illness, his popularity began to dwindle. Unless he addressed this animal infection, he would not be reelected, but most importantly, this animal carrying disease would spread to nearby states and all across America if not caught in time. The result would be the death of millions of Americans.

The governor was shocked by this interpretation. He responded immediately to Joseph's interpretation. The governor had no clue about the seriousness of this outbreak within the farming community although farmers and agriculturalists tried to bring it to his attention. The governor did not want to spend additional money to address the situation. His advisors assured him this would pass.

The governor was escorted out of the room and went straight to his office to make some important phone calls to persons on his staff who were connected to both the health and farming policies in his administration. After several phone calls and scheduling meetings for the rest of the week, the governor began to ponder about who could oversee a commission to study and respond to this health crisis. In the meantime, Joseph was returned to his prison cell.

A meeting was held a 2-days later with his aides. It was suggested that Joseph be appointed as the head of the commission. After all, it was Joseph who was able to interpret the governor's dream. (After the interpretation the governor slept like a baby). The governor's lawyer reminded him of how well the warden spoke of Joseph. In addition, the lawyer remembered that he promised to look into Joseph's case to see if he was given a fair trial, since he was convicted from the testimony of only one person. (It was later proven that this woman had an axe to grind because Joseph would not give in to her sexual advances). *(Gen 39:14-18)*

So the governor had his Attorney General review the evidence of the case and found that Joseph was innocent. The woman recanted her original testimony. Instead of granting Joseph a new trial, all charges against Joseph were dropped and he was set free. Now he could serve as the head of the governor's commission on the infection of animals on the farms in his state. Unfortunately the media did not cover his innocence. If the story made the news maybe his family would have seen the coverage and realized what happened to Joseph and where he was for the last 10 years.

Since this outbreak of infected animals was occurring in a large city, no one really knew anything about Joseph or his background. He had aged 20 years and looked nothing like the 17-year old kid falsely accused of a crime. In addition, Joseph did not want to take credit away from the governor's efforts so he avoided the spotlight and remained in the background.

Because the governor was able to catch this infection early, and respond quickly, it was under control in a matter of 6 months. A quick response saved the lives of many people and thousands of livestock across the country especially in the farming community. Joseph's interpretation saved the day, but it was not over yet.

The animals that were infected had to be put down so they would not contaminate other animals and continue the spread of the disease. This meant that there would be a temporary meat shortage across the state. How would Joseph and his staff address this shortage? What would it cost the state to replenish the livestock of farmers with enough animals that their financial bottom lines would not be affected and they could still make a profit?

Joseph and his staff decided to advertise for the need of healthy livestock. The governor set up a line item on the budget to financially address this need. The disease outbreak seemed to be contained just in this state. Or so they thought. What they discovered was that this disease did not stop at the state border.

Unknown to Joseph back home his father's flocks were also infected by this disease. His family had already lost 100 head of cattle and at least 50 more may have been infected. His brothers were trying to separate the healthy cattle from the sick ones, but it was a challenge because of their foolery, they had not paid close enough attention to when the animals first showed signs of the disease. The family was just praying now that they would not loose their entire livelihood to this horrible disease.

The disease did not seem to spread as far as the northeastern section of the country. Joseph and his staff were able to purchase 1000 head of cattle and goats from the north. They were very careful not to allow the newly purchased animals to come in contact with the suspected diseased cattle. The new cattle were located on the other side of the state where the disease was still nonexistent. This strategy allowed the governor to maintain a healthy and disease-free meat chain supply.

CHAPTER 6

Joseph Turns His Challenge Into A Family Reunion (Genesis 42-46)

nfortunately some southern regions did not use this strategy. Many states denied the seriousness of the disease until it was too late and many of their farmers lost everything! They turned the health crisis into a political debate. When neighboring states heard about what Joseph was dong to protect the cattle in his region, they too began sending representatives to meet with Joseph. They received advice and were allowed to purchase new disease-free cattle.

JOSEPH AND HIS BROTHERS MEET AFTER 20 YEARS (GENESIS 43:1-34)

On one such visit, Joseph's brothers arrived to purchase cattle for their farm back home. Many of their flocks were victim to this deadly disease and their father, Jacob, sent them to Joseph's state to purchase new cattle in order to replenish their cattle supply. By now Joseph had been gone from home for almost 20 years. When his brothers last saw him he was just a scrawny teenager. Now he was a grown man with matured features that changed his appearance greatly.

Therefore, when they came to Joseph to request the purchase of cattle, they did not even recognize Joseph! Oh but Joseph recognized them! *(Gen 42:8)* When he saw the faces of the 3 brothers who put him in a well, and never came to bail him out of jail, his heart sank and the pain he was able to suppress all these many years surfaced. What they had done to Joseph was cruel and hateful to do to anyone no less one's own flesh and blood!

Joseph never forgot what his brothers did to him and how they deprived him of his father's embrace and love for 20 years. His first thought was to punish them and get revenge. So Joseph began to plot revenge against his brothers so they would get a taste of their own medicine. Joseph did not want to do them any physical harm; he just wanted to teach them a lesson. *(Gen 44:1-5)*

Joseph decided to set his brothers up for a theft charge. When they paid the treasurer for the 50 head of cattle they loaded on their trailer, Joseph would have one of his assistants plant the funds back in the glove compartment of the truck that pulled the trailer. The money would be discovered as they tried to leave the premises. *(Gen 44:1-2)*

Sure enough, everything went down the way Joseph planned. After his 3 brothers paid for the 50 head of cattle, they returned to their truck to leave. The cattle were loaded and the brothers got in the truck and headed for home. There was one last checkpoint they had to go through before they could leave the farm. As they approached the final checkpoint, the guard stopped them. The brothers were bewildered because they knew they had followed all the rules.

The guard at the booth approached the older brother, Reuben. Reuben asked the guard what was the problem. The guard told Reuben an anonymous tip had come in just now accusing them of not paying for the cattle in their trailer. Reuben said that was not true and reached into the glove compartment to retrieve his receipt. When he opened the glove compartment, all the money fell out that they brought to purchase the cattle. They smelled a set up but had no proof. Who would do this to them? *(Gen 44:8)*

The guard immediately arrested the 3 brothers and charged them with theft. They were taken to the local jail until this misunderstanding could be cleared up. Sound familiar? Twenty years ago to this exact date, Joseph was falsely accused and arrested on trumped up charges. He was put in a jail cell without any explanation. Karma was truly the order of the day. *(Gen 44:17)*

After a couple of days of incarceration, Joseph had a change of heart. His assistant called the jail and had his brothers brought to him. They were relieved to finally get out of jail, but still had no idea what had happened. As they waited for Joseph to appear in his office, the brothers were trying to figure out what they were going to say. Had they been exonerated? Pardoned? Did the receipt suddenly reappear? What in the world was going on?

Joseph arrived to his office about 15 minutes after the brothers. Joseph wanted to let them sit for a while just to get one last ounce of revenge out of his system. He wanted them to feel the pain he felt when they set him up to be arrested because of their jealousy towards him. But Joseph's heart was not as hard as his 3 brothers'. Even though they put him through a lot of pain and suffering, and lost time with his father, Joseph could still see the hand of God in the situation.

———————————

FORGIVENESS CANCELS VENGEANCE (GENESIS 45:1-8)

When Joseph walked in the office he began telling a story about a young boy who was very much loved by his father. Joseph continued with details about his life as a child and how his mother died giving birth to his younger brother. Joseph then mentioned he had 10 older brothers who did not like him because of the favoritism their father showed towards him, and the close bond he had with his father. His father used to send him to the fields to check on his older brothers to make sure they were getting the job done and not slacking off.

Joseph's story gave more and more details and the 3 brothers were beginning to notice the similarity between Joseph's story and their family history. Joseph added more details about how he was falsely accused of a crime and that none of his family members cared enough to come to his rescue.

This travesty of justice could have made him bitter, but Joseph stated that God assured him all that he was experiencing was in his will. So although initially vengeance was sweet, even when served cold, he realized God would want him to forgive his brothers and become reconciled with them.

At this moment, Joseph revealed his identity to his brothers. He got up f rom his office hair and looked them straight in their eyes and said, "It is I, your brother Joseph." The brothers were shocked. They did not know if they should cry or laugh, hug Joseph or run for the door! They stood frozen in their seats waiting for some direction from Joseph on how they should respond. *(Gen 45:4)*

Joseph began to cry and express his sorrow for their actions against him. Then he laughed and opened his arms signaling they were forgiven and all is well. The brothers threw their arms around Joseph and expressed how deeply sorry they were for neglecting and rejecting him all these many years. *(Gen 45:1, 2, 15)*

Joseph let them know that even though what they did was meant to destroy him and erase him from their father's heart, they failed. God used him to predict this disease crisis in the region through his gift of interpretation of dreams. The governor had a dream no one could interpret, but him. This prevented a possible epidemic that would have destroyed millions of farm animals across the country. *(Gen 45:8)*

Joseph forgave them and after tears and hugs, Joseph wanted to know how his father was doing. Was he still alive? How about his little brother Benjamin? Surely he was a grown man now. Did he have a family? Joseph's brothers assured him that both were doing fine. Their father never gave up hope that he would see Joseph again. His heart was broken into pieces by their jealousy and actions against Joseph. He prayed to the God of his ancestors for Joseph's safe return at least 3 times a day. Watching Jacob pine over Joseph made their guilt even worse. Seeing Joseph again will be like a new lease on life for Jacob. *(Gen 37:34-35; 44:9-15, 27-28))*

A FAMILY REUNION (GENESIS 46)

Joseph instructed his brothers to go back home and tell their father his son was very much alive. A phone call would be too much of a shocker. So Joseph's 3 brothers left Joseph's side and returned home to their father. When he heard the news he wanted to see Joseph for himself. A phone call was not enough. So they packed their elderly father and Benjamin in the car and droved to meet Joseph in person at his place of residence.

When the car arrived a few hours later, Jacob got out of the car. Joseph met his father at the front door. Jacob could not believe his aging eyes. Was this his beloved son Joseph? Was this his firstborn son with his beloved Rachael? The tears and hugs were non-stop for almost 30 minutes. Joseph helped his aged father into his home and shared the story of his life over the past 20 years.

At times Jacob wept, not realizing how his favoritism towards Joseph and Benjamin negatively impacted his other children. He was just so heartbroken over the lost of his beloved Rachael, the only woman he ever loved, that he became over protective of her offspring. He never meant to offend or withhold his love from his other children. Life just seemed to happen that way.

The other children never openly complained to Jacob about their feelings, but they certainly let Joseph know. On a few occasions, Joseph shared his brothers' disdain toward him with Jacob, but Jacob having experienced sibling rivalry with his twin brother Esau, just shrugged it off thinking the boys would work it out eventually. Even though he had not worked things out with Esau over the past 40 years. *(Gen 33:15-17)*

The irony of the two situations was too close for comfort. Maybe it is true that the sins of the father fall on the son. *(Exo 20:5)* The reunion was meant to heal past wounds or so Joseph thought. Seventeen years after his family relocated to Joseph's city, Jacob died. He was taken back to Canaan and buried in the family plot alongside his beloved Rachael. Now they would be together forever. *(Gen 49:7-14, 33)*

Joseph took Jacob's death really hard. He had lost so much time with his father because of his brothers' animosity towards him. In a moment of grief and anger, Joseph's first emotion was to hate his brothers. But Joseph's heart for God would not allow that moment to linger and Joseph instead moved from anger to gratitude for the life he was living today. God used him to avoid a major catastrophe that may have resulted in millions of dead livestock and countless human lives. *(Gen 49:19-20)*

Looking back over his life, Joseph had no regrets. Yes, he would have preferred not be falsely accused and thrown in prison for 10 years, but overall life turned out pretty good because no matter what the circumstances or conditions, God was with Joseph the whole time. Joseph married the governor's daughter and they had 2 sons.

Jacob blessed all his sons and both of Joseph's sons before he died. Joseph was filled with gratitude that God allowed him to be reunited with his father before he died. Now his relationship with his siblings was better than ever. *(Gen 48:14-16)* Things were looking up. In the words of the Psalmist: *"I will lift mine eyes unto the hills, from whence comes my help? My help comes from the Lord who made heaven and earth.... The Lord shall preserve your soul. The Lord shall preserve your going out and your coming in from this time forth, and even for evermore."* *(Ps 121:1-2, 7-8, KJV)*

Amen, amen, amen!

Printed in the United States
by Baker & Taylor Publisher Services